A Smile from Andy

By Nan Holcomb

Illustrated by Dot Yoder

JASON & NORDIC PUBLISHERS
EXTON, PENNSYLVANIA

Other Turtle Books

Patrick and Emma Lou
Andy finds a Turtle
Danny and the Merry-Go-Round
How About a Hug

Library of Congress Cataloging-in-Publication Data

Holcomb, Nan, date-
  A smile from Andy / by Nan Holcomb ; illustrated by Dot Yoder.
    p.   cm.
  Summary: A child with cerebral palsy is hindered in meeting new people by his shyness, until he discovers the special thing he can do to make people feel like talking to him.
    ISBN 0-944727-04-2
    [1. Cerebral palsy — Fiction.   2. Physically handicapped — Fiction.]
  I. Yoder, Dot, date-   ill.   II. Title.
  PZ7.H6972Sm   1989
  [E] — dc20

                                                            89-34596
                                                              CIP
                                                              AC

ISBN 0-944727-04-2
Printed in the U.S.A.

A new word from Andy!
GRIM — is the way you feel when you are not
sad enough to cry, happy enough to smile,
angry enough to scream. It feels just like it
sounds — grrrimmm!

Andy felt shy.
Andy felt grim.
Andy wanted people to talk to him.

"Come, Andy. Let's get this jacket on.
We're going for a walk," Mommy said.

Mommy pushed Andy in his special chair with wheels. Grandma pushed Baby Sue in her stroller.

When people walked by, Andy didn't know what to do. He stared at the trees. . .

or if people stopped, he stared at their knees.

Andy felt shy.
Andy felt grim.
Andy wanted people to talk to him.

They stopped at the bank. The bank lady said, "Hi!" Baby Sue laughed and bounced up and down. The lady said, "My, you're a cute little girl."

Andy felt shy so he closed his eyes tight.
The bank lady looked at him and said, "He's
certainly a sleepy-head." Then she tickled
Sue under the chin.

Andy felt **grim.** He wanted the lady to
talk to him.

They walked to the mall. Sue goo-gooed at an old lady resting on the bench. Andy felt shy so he closed his eyes tight.

The old lady said, "His eyes are closed tight. Must be he didn't sleep much last night." Then she tickled Sue under the chin.

Andy felt **terribly grim.** He wanted people to talk to him.

At the bakery Mom met a school friend who had twins. One was named Tom and the other was Tim.

Andy closed his eyes — but not very tight. He could just see through the crack. When the twins looked at him, he didn't look back.

Tom stood on his head and yelled,
"Mom, look at me! I'm a clown — upside
down!"

Andy opened his eyes a bit wider and
looked through a much bigger crack.

Tim grabbed his Mom's skirt and started sucking his thumb. He started to whine a very loud whine.

"Tim hasn't learned to be a clown — upside down — and he certainly isn't happy about it," Tim's mother explained. Tim tugged her skirt harder and whined even louder.

Andy thought, Hmm-m-m. My feet aren't in the air. They aren't even on the ground. My feet stay flat, right in my chair and I'm not very happy about that! Andy whined and thought about sucking his thumb, but that looked pretty dumb.

The mothers both said, "That's enough from you two. Nobody likes to hear boys whine. It will just never do."

Andy felt grim. That wasn't the kind of talking he had in mind! That just wasn't the kind! He was almost glad when Mom said, "Good-by, Tom. Good-by, Tim."

He was very glad when Grandma said,
"Who's hungry? Let's eat right here in the
mall."

Andy liked to eat under the trees. He
looked up through the leaves to the roof of

the mall. He wondered if they would ever grow that tall.

He forgot he was shy. He forgot he felt grim. He opened his eyes and watched everything.

The pizza man tossed pizza dough high in the air and twirled it around. When people clapped, he smiled and took a bow.

The pizza man didn't feel shy. He didn't feel grim. People all clapped and talked to him.

The balloon man walked by and winked his eye at the flower lady. She smiled and waved a rose at him.

The flower lady didn't look shy and she didn't look grim. She laughed out loud and threw the flower to him!

Andy thought, maybe if I could twirl a pizza or sell balloons or even throw a rose... just maybe people would stop and talk to me. Just then...

he saw her! A little red-headed girl stood in front of him. She looked like a wise owl staring at him through big round glasses.

He stared right back.

Her curls bounced in bunches like red floppy ears when she turned around fast and leaned over to Sue.

She took Sue's hands and said, "Hi, little girl. What's your name? My name's Liz."

Sue bounced and goo-gooed as she always did.

Before Andy could shut his eyes, be shy
or grim, the little girl bounced back to him.
She grabbed his hand and said, "Hi! Your
name's Andy! I read it right there on your
chair! My name's Liz!"

He looked right at her great big grin and smiled his best smile. He opened his big blue eyes that almost nobody had ever seen — and just beamed!

"You look happy when you smile and you make me feel happy, too. Look everbody! Andy's happy!

Andy smiled again. He didn't feel shy
and he didn't feel grim.

Everyone gathered around, laughed and talked with him.

I can't stand on my head or walk or swim... but... I'll never feel grim again! Now, when I'm shy, I'll just grin a BIG GRIN!